ADVENTURES

Sinbad
and the Monkeys

by Martin Waddell and O'Kif

W

FRANKLIN WATTS
LONDON•SYDNEY

First published in 2009 by
Franklin Watts
338 Euston Road
London
NW1 3BH

Franklin Watts Australia
Level 17/207 Kent Street
Sydney
NSW 2000

A CIP catalogue record for this book is available
from the British Library.

ISBN 978 0 7496 8560 7 (hbk)
ISBN 978 0 7496 8572 0 (pbk)

Series Editor: Jackie Hamley
Series Advisor: Dr Barrie Wade
Series Designer: Peter Scoulding

Printed in China

Franklin Watts is a division of
Hachette Children's Books,
an Hachette UK company
www.hachette.co.uk

One day, Sinbad's crew rowed back
to his ship with a huge egg.

"A roc's egg!" Sinbad said sharply.
"Get it off my ship!"

"What's a roc?" asked Ali.

"That is!" yelled Sinbad.

Two gigantic, angry rocs
dive-bombed the ship with
big stones until it sank.

Sinbad and Ali escaped in a small boat. They rowed all day to the Island of Monkeys.

"We'll have to shake coconuts
from the trees," Ali told Sinbad.
"There's nothing else to eat."

"The monkeys are dangerous
here!" warned Sinbad.

"I don't see any monkeys,"
said Ali, then...

BIFF BASH BOP! BIFF BOP BASH!

"Ouch!" wailed Ali as a coconut bounced off his head.

"Take cover! Monkey attack!"
yelled Sinbad.
"Take cover where?" groaned Ali.

"Turn the boat upside-down and hide underneath!" said Sinbad.

"Either we starve to death or we get battered to bits by fierce monkeys!" groaned Ali. "How do we get out of this?"

"Think, think, THINK!" Sinbad said. And he thought...

And he thought...

"We invent the Sinbad-and-Ali-Land-Turtle!" smiled Sinbad.

Sinbad took the nets and oars and fixed them to the upturned boat. "You be the back turtle legs. I'll be the front," Sinbad told Ali.

"I don't like this idea," shivered Ali. "Bring on the monkeys. Let them do their worst!" laughed Sinbad.

The Sinbad-and-Ali-Land-Turtle moved up from the shore, very slowly. "Now for the monkey attack!" Sinbad whispered and...

BIFF BASH BOP! BIFF BOP BASH!
The monkeys attacked. Soon the
nets were coconut-filled.

The Sinbad-and-Ali-Land-Turtle
turned towards the beach, with a
horde of fierce monkeys chasing it.
The monkeys were catching up fast.

"Quick Ali!" said Sinbad, dodging
the coconut fire. They righted the
boat and set off to sea with a
cargo of coconuts.

"No one makes a monkey of me!"
Sinbad boasted. Then...

BOP!

A coconut bounced off his head.

"Tough luck, Sinbad!" grinned Ali.

Before long, a ship rescued them. Sinbad sold the coconuts to the ship's captain for a bag of gold and tickets for their journey home.

"That was good monkey business!"
laughed Sinbad the Sailor.

Puzzle 1

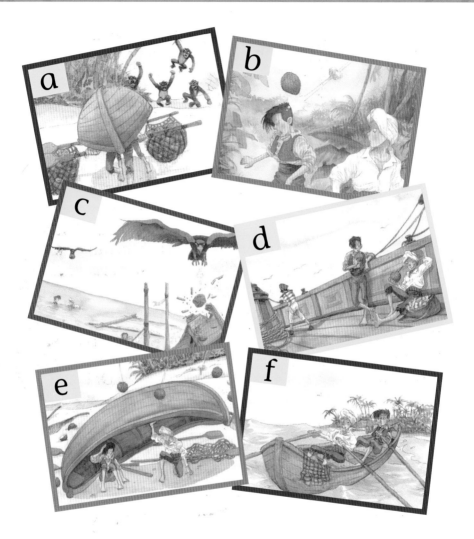

Put these pictures in the correct order.
Which event do you think is most important?
Now try writing the story in your own words!

1. I've heard about these monkeys.

2. Look what we found in a nest.

3. I see no monkeys.

4. Why do I have to be the back legs?

5. Help us get this on the ship!

6. I'm not having that on board my ship!

Choose the correct speech bubbles for the characters above. Can you think of any others? Turn over to find the answers.

Answers

Puzzle 1

The correct order is: 1c, 2f, 3b, 4e, 5a, 6d

Puzzle 2

Sinbad: 1, 6

Ali: 3, 4

The sailors: 2, 5

Look out for more Hopscotch Adventures:

For more *Hopscotch Adventures* and other *Hopscotch* stories, visit:
www.franklinwatts.co.uk

* hardback